KEEPER
CRYSTALS

Eve and the Runaway Unicorn

For Elkie, who wished
for her own unicorn.

First published in the UK in 2017.
This edition published in 2019
by New Frontier Publishing Pty Ltd
Uncommon, 126 New King's Rd, Fulham SW6 4LZ
www.newfrontierpublishing.co.uk

ISBN: 978-0-9956255-7-0 (PB)

A CIP catalogue record for this book is available from the British Library.

Designed by Celeste Hulme

Printed in China
10 9 8 7 6 5 4 3 2

KEEPER OF THE
CRYSTALS

Eve and the Runaway Unicorn

Jess Black
Illustrated by Celeste Hulme

ve wanted to play dress-ups. Oscar was having none of it. He had gone along with her when it meant dressing as a ninja pirate. But when she announced they were forming an all-girl princess band, he put his ninja-slippered foot down and refused.

'In case you haven't noticed, I'm *not* a girl.' Oscar adopted a fighting ninja stance.

'A minor detail,' scoffed Eve as she handed him a pop-star outfit covered in purple sequins. 'Try this on.'

Oscar glared at her. He waved his arms around, cutting through the air like a ninja on the attack. Then he flew into the air and landed in a crouch position, glaring up at her.

'Come *on*!' Eve exclaimed, swishing around in her most princessy of princess dresses. 'It'll be heaps of fun!'

'No way!' glowered Oscar. 'The master of shadows does not wear a dress.'

Eve glanced down at the dress she was wearing. What was there not to love? It had sparkles. It had tulle. It was pink and it was very swirly. Eve loved going through her gran's old dresses when she visited. She had a vintage dress collection which took up an entire cupboard! Eve had even rummaged through her gran's costume jewellery and found some diamond-drop earrings and matching bracelet because they were especially sparkly.

Not that there was anybody at 48 Clearview Street to notice. Eve was stuck with only one playmate under the age of eighty. His name was Oscar. He and his family lived next door to her gran. Eve wondered what he did out here. The small town where her gran lived was so quiet and full of old people. It was nothing like the big city where Eve lived.

'Oh, come on,' pleaded Eve, 'can't you see I'm desperate?'

'No!' Oscar crossed his arms and frowned at her.

'Yes!' countered Eve, doing a twirl and coming to a halt in front of him. As Eve practised her ballet points she studied him.

3

He was still scowling.

Oscar might as well have come from another planet. He looked perfectly normal at first glance: straggly brown hair, a little on the skinny side, a few freckles on his nose. But he was an alien being. He was a *boy*.

As though reading her mind Oscar said, 'What planet do you come from? I'm a boy. I don't do dresses.' He threw the pop-star dress at Eve. It landed at her feet in a glittery pile.

'Careful!' Eve picked up the dress and carefully folded it in her arms. 'This is vintage.'

'Smells like mothballs,' muttered Oscar.

Eve rolled her eyes. She pouted her bottom lip. She humphed. But her diva act had zero effect on the ninja. He danced away, fighting off imaginary evil baddies. Soon he was out the front door and heading up the brick path to his house. Eve sighed. What was it about boys? They were so ... She struggled to think of the right word. *Impossible?*

'Oh, that's right, just abandon me,' she yelled at Oscar's retreating back. 'Everyone else has!'

Oscar didn't answer or turn around. He was practising his ninja punch followed by an air kick. Eve watched as he fell onto the grass and landed on his bottom. She laughed quietly to herself.

What am I doing here? Eve asked herself for the tenth time that day. Her parents had dropped her at her gran's house and taken off on holiday with hardly a backwards glance. A *cruise!* Just thinking about it made Eve's blood boil. What kind of parent goes on holiday without their child?

To be fair, Eve's gran was really lovely and

she was very kind to Eve.

But she was so *old*. Right now she was having her afternoon nap and Eve had no other option than Oscar. But he was a boy, and Eve was pretty sure that they didn't like each other much at all.

Eve had a choice. She could keep playing on her own or play with the ninja.

She gave in and clomped over to his house (as much as you can clomp while wearing plastic heels). He was sitting on his front steps.

'What would *you* like to do?' Eve asked in a small voice. She tried not to sound too keen.

Oscar perked up. 'Didn't you say that your gran had a cool attic?'

'Y–e–s … ' Eve replied hesitantly. At the thought of the attic she felt a tingle run through her fingers and toes. Under no circumstances was she allowed in the attic. It was the only rule her gran had and it went something like: 'You are NEVER to go into the attic, Eve. Do we have an UNDERSTANDING?'

'Let's check it out,' Oscar suggested brightly.

Eve thought for a moment. 'Okay,' she agreed, 'but we'll have to be super silent. If my gran finds out I am dead meat.'

'I'd hate for that to happen,' Oscar replied with a cheeky smile.

Eve didn't know if he meant it or not. What she did know was that her stomach was doing flips and that she was about to do something really thrilling that might get her and Oscar into trouble. But at least they were doing something exciting!

Eve couldn't wait!

'You're scared!' whispered Oscar as he shot Eve a scornful look.

'Am not!' Eve hissed back.

They were standing outside her gran's bedroom door, which was slightly ajar. Her soft snores could be heard from out in the hall. Eve knew the key to the attic door was kept in a small silver box by her gran's bed.

'I smell mothballs again,' said Oscar wrinkling his nose. 'Go on then.' He jerked his head towards the bedroom. 'Or have you chickened out?'

Eve ignored him and gently pushed the door open wide enough to slink inside. As always she was welcomed by the aroma of talcum powder and lavender. She loved her gran's room, with its muted colours and soft edges.

Eve tiptoed over to the bedside table and opened the silver trinket box with shaking fingers. She carefully picked up the small brass key and replaced the lid. Her gran's face looked so peaceful and she seemed to be deeply asleep. 'Sorry,' Eve mouthed to the sleeping figure as she backed out of the room.

She took Oscar down the hall, showing him the ladder that led to the attic.

'Let me go first,' said Oscar as he brushed past Eve and with ninja stealth he scaled the rungs in no time.

'Fine,' muttered Eve. She scooped up the extra material on her long dress and tucked it under one arm, then followed Oscar up the ladder. He had already reached the small trapdoor at the top of the ladder. The door was locked.

Eve handed the key to Oscar and watched anxiously as it turned in the keyhole, giving a satisfying clunk as it unlocked.

'Alright!' Oscar exclaimed as he pushed open the door and disappeared into the gloom beyond. With one last glance at her gran's open bedroom door Eve followed Oscar into the attic.

**

It was very dark inside the attic except for tiny shards of light streaming up through the cracks in the floorboards. The room smelled musty and mouldy.

'This place is *awesome!*' said Oscar.

'Shhh!' said Eve. 'You'll wake Gran!'

Oscar switched on the torch app on his phone and a bright beam revealed a pile of dusty boxes against one wall. Oscar moved the torch slowly around the room, revealing an old metal chest, a lacquered wooden box that looked Chinese, more piles of boxes and stacks of newspapers.

'It's creepy, that's for sure,' said Eve in a low voice. She shuddered as she heard the scritch scratch of rats scuttling away from the intruders.

Oscar took a closer look at a newspaper on top of a pile.

'Check out the date.' He pointed to the

11

front page and held the torch onto it so they could read.

'1937! That's so old.' Eve ran her hand gingerly over the old paper. It felt delicate and soft and her fingers tingled as she held it. She scanned the headlines on the front page and something twigged in her memory. '24th of May 1937,' she read aloud. 'That's my gran's birthday and the year she was born!'

'Spooky!' said Oscar. He moved away and took the light source with him. 'Hey, check this out.'

Eve joined Oscar who was kneeling in front of the large metal chest. It was firmly locked with a large steel padlock. This told Eve two things: one, that there was something important inside that she simply had to see; and two, that they would have to find a way to unlock it.

'Shall we open it?' Eve whispered.

Oscar looked doubtful. 'Your call.'

'Yes!' exclaimed Eve a little too loudly. She lowered her voice. 'But how?'

'I can try ... ' said Oscar. He pulled a small leather pouch from his pocket and opened it. Inside was a silver Swiss Army knife.

'You really are a ninja,' Eve commented, impressed.

'Boys have their uses,' Oscar muttered. He opened and shut various tools from the knife before deciding a screwdriver was the right one for the job.

Oscar jiggled the pointy end of the screwdriver in the lock. The padlock itself was rusty and after a bit of fiddling Eve heard a tiny click. Oscar glanced at her with a big grin before he slid the padlock open. It fell to the floor with a clunk.

'Show-off,' Eve whispered, 'although I

13

have to admit that was pretty cool.'

The lid of the chest was very heavy and even with both of them pushing they strained to open it.

'Let's put some muscle into it,' whispered Eve.

They gave one last big push. The lid lifted and they leaned it carefully against the wall. Eve peered inside while Oscar held his torch.

'It's full of old curtains,' Eve said, disappointed, as she ran her hands through metres of heavy purple velvet.

'What did you expect?' Oscar chuckled. 'It's your gran's attic.'

Eve's hand caught on something heavy at the base of the chest. 'Hang on!'

She felt that strange sensation again, her hands felt tingly and hot. She lifted a small parcel from the base of the trunk. It was wrapped in red tissue paper. With trembling fingers Eve unwrapped it to reveal a small crystal figurine. It was a unicorn slightly smaller than the palm of her hand. The crystal gleamed under the torchlight and projected little rainbows of light around the attic.

'It's gorgeous!' Eve gasped.

'It's kind of cool, I guess,' said Oscar in a voice which suggested it was anything but.

Eve cradled the little unicorn in her hand and held it up for a closer look. It was the most magnificent treasure and beautifully made. The unicorn had its head held high. The crystal caught the light of the torch and sparkled. Fragments of light spun around the room like fireflies.

'Eve, something weird is happening.'

Eve could do nothing but watch, entranced. The fractals of light were bouncing off the unicorn as if it was a huge mirror ball. It was magical.

'Put that thing down,' Oscar warned.

'I can't.' Eve couldn't move. She was too captivated by the light, by the power of the unicorn.

Oscar lunged at the crystal to swipe it from Eve's grasp but he was too late.

The entire room was flooded with white light.

$\mathcal{E}$ ve was falling.

At first she thought the ceiling must have collapsed and she braced herself for the landing. But the landing didn't come. She was sinking so fast that her stomach felt like it was in her mouth. All she could see was a bright light. She continued falling and turning through bright fluffy clouds. Her dark curls flew around her head in a tangle and her arms flailed as she plunged through the air, falling faster and faster.

Then it was over.

Eve felt no thud or pain but when she opened her eyes she was lying on the ground.

'What the ... ?' She sat up with a start. She was no longer in the attic. She was lying on her back in warm sand in what looked like a desert. The clouds were up in the sky again, far out of her reach.

Eve felt the gritty sand between her fingers. 'The unicorn ... '

What had happened to the crystal figurine she had been holding? She opened her hand. The unicorn was no longer there but it had left a perfect unicorn-shaped imprint on her palm. A flurry of sand caught her eye and she thought she saw a white horse cantering away in the distance.

'Where are we?' asked a voice.

Eve scrambled up onto her knees to see Oscar standing behind her. She had forgotten all about him. His cheeks were flushed and he looked scared.

'I have no idea,' Eve answered in a small voice. One minute they were in a dark attic and the next they were under hot sun in a desert. She searched for landmarks but saw only multi-coloured layers of sand stretching to the horizon.

'I've lost the unicorn.' Eve searched through the sand around her.

'We've got bigger things to worry about than some trinket,' said Oscar. He checked his phone. It had no service at all. Not even SOS. He showed the blank screen to Eve.

'What are we going to do?' she asked.

Oscar shrugged. 'Walk?'

Oscar and Eve walked aimlessly across endless sandhills. Eve's dress was soon drenched in sweat. The shiny material wasn't made for spontaneous desert treks and Eve was sorry she was wearing it.

'I'd give anything for a smoothie right now,' joked Oscar.

Eve groaned at the thought. 'Or a chocolate thickshake!'

They shared a brief smile and pushed on. At the top of the next rise they were welcomed by more sand dunes and a hazy honey-coloured horizon which shimmered and danced.

Eve pointed to a pool of ice-blue water in the near distance. 'Is that a mirage?'

'It's real all right,' said Oscar. They broke

into a run, almost falling over themselves to get to the waterhole. Eve kneeled before the pool and plunged her hands into its cool depths. Just as the water was about to touch Eve's lips she was startled by a loud voice.

'Stop!'

Eve and Oscar swung around to see a figure completely swathed in layers of sand-coloured material. Eve let the water trickle through her fingers onto the sand. She stood close to Oscar who put a protective arm in front of her.

'The water here is not safe to drink,' the stranger explained in a more gentle tone.

'Where are we?' Oscar asked.

'This is the desert of Panthor,' the stranger answered.

'Right,' sighed Oscar, 'and where is that?'

'Near the Borderlands,' came the answer.

Neither of the names rang a bell. 'We're

lost. We're not from around here,' Eve explained.

'I can tell.' The stranger gave a small smile and pointed to their outfits.

Eve thought furiously. She was good at geography and couldn't remember ever hearing about Panthor or the Borderlands in class. She clenched her hands into fists and then opened them again. The mark on her palm was still there.

The stranger gasped and pointed at Eve's open palm. 'What's that mark on your hand?'

Eve glanced at Oscar before replying. 'I'm not sure. I was holding a unicorn crystal when we arrived here and it's left this on my hand.'

The stranger's eyes grew wide. 'I need to get you to safety.'

'Who are you?' asked Oscar.

The stranger unwrapped the silk from around her eyes and revealed her face. She was a young girl slightly older than Eve. 'My name is Callie.'

'I'm E–' Eve began.

'I know who you are,' interrupted Callie. 'You are the one we have been waiting for.'

'The one! As if!' muttered Oscar as he trudged up another sand dune beside Eve and Callie. Eve glanced at him and shrugged. It all seemed just as strange to her.

As they walked, Callie told them about her world. Even Oscar, for all his grumbling, started to look interested.

'This wasn't always desert,' she explained. 'We used to have trees, plants, birds, lush forest. But everything changed when the Borderlands were taken over. 'We were cast out to the fringes. We're known as outliers.'

'Who is doing this?' Oscar asked. He'd fallen behind checking his phone but the battery had died. He caught up with the girls.

'The king. He is greedy. He wants more land. He wants to control everything. The animals are caged. The plants are left to die. Some people say he is crazy.' She waved a hand in the air. 'What can we do? We are not fighters. We live in harmony with the animals and the land.'

'Tell me more about the prophecy,' Oscar prompted her.

Callie smiled shyly. 'I always thought it was a story they told to children at bedtime, just a story, but … it goes like this. *A girl with curls as black as the night will meet one fair as light.'*

Callie stopped walking and unwrapped the cloth from around her head. Her curls escaped from the binding and tumbled down to rest on her shoulders. Her hair was white blonde, as fair as Eve's was dark.

'There could be heaps of strangers with black hair that fit the story,' objected Oscar.

'Jealous?' Eve raised an eyebrow.

Callie continued:

'They will meet where water is no more
That is the time of the great war.
One will come with the mark of unicorn
The land of Panthor will be reborn'.

'O-*kay*,' joked Oscar, 'that is a little creepy.' He shot Eve a meaningful look.

Eve cleared her throat before speaking, 'The mark on my hand is from holding a glass unicorn, and it's not permanent.'

'You need to talk to my parents,' said Callie. 'We're nearly there.'

Eve gazed down at her hand. The mark was still there. It was as fresh as when she had first laid eyes on it.

Callie resumed walking. Oscar trotted after her. 'Did the prophecy say anything about a boy named Oscar?'

***

Callie's community lived in simple homes made from mudbricks. They looked like igloos, built low to the ground and blending in perfectly with the surrounding environment.

'We used to live in treehouses, but now there are no more trees. Life is very different.' Callie disappeared inside one of the domes and came out with two hollow seed pods filled to the brim with water.

'I need to find my parents,' Callie said. 'Stay here and rest.'

She led Eve and Oscar to a shadecloth strung between two of the domes. They sank exhausted onto the cool ground and gulped down their water. It tasted gritty but it was water and they were both very thirsty.

'Do you think our parents have sent out a search party?' Oscar asked.

Eve hated to think how worried her gran would be. 'I guess so. Gran will have to track down Mum and Dad on their cruise.' She felt terrible. Her parents would rush home immediately from their holiday.

They sat in silence until Callie returned with her mother and father. They too had white blonde hair like Callie's which stood out against their olive skin.

'I am Thern and this is Mild,' Callie's father said, giving the kids a solemn bow. 'You are welcome here. We have been waiting for you for a long time.'

'This is Oscar and my name is Eve,' said Eve, a little flustered, 'but there's been some mistake. We're just two kids.'

Thern looked at them thoughtfully. 'You are the key to freeing our land. You see, our animals have always looked to one creature: the unicorn.'

'But unicorns don't really exist,' Eve argued.

'Ah, but they do.' Thern waggled a finger at Eve. 'You brought the unicorn here which means you have a very rare power.'

'Now that I think about it, I did see an animal that looked like a unicorn canter away. I thought it was a horse … ' Eve trailed off.

29

Thern and Mild grew excited. 'The unicorn is the only animal that the people of Panthor haven't been able to speak to. We are able to live in harmony with all wild animals here but not the unicorns. They live on the fringes and keep to themselves.'

Eve and Oscar shared a look.

'Where the unicorn has gone will be very dangerous. You will go with Ibid.' Thern clapped his hands together and it seemed the matter was settled.

'Who's Ibid?' Oscar whispered to Callie.

Callie pointed to the entrance of one of the dwellings. At the sound of the clap, out walked an enormous black panther.

Eve sucked in her breath. The panther fixed his huge yellow eyes on her and stalked towards her.

*S*tanding beside Callie, the panther came up to her chest. Eve was tall for her age, and she and the cat eyeballed each other. His powerful muscles rippled beneath his thick black coat. Two huge eyes locked on Eve with an eerie intensity.

Oscar pushed Eve forwards. 'You're the *one*,' he murmured. 'Deal with it.'

'Nice k–k–kitty,' Eve stammered. She was too scared to move.

'There is no need to be alarmed,' Thern assured them. 'Our people communicate with animals through our thoughts. Ibid is my animal guide. He will protect you.'

'If you say so,' said Oscar in a low voice. 'Hi Ibid.' He gave the panther a half-hearted wave but stood firmly behind Eve.

'Could the unicorn have gone to the lakes of Trapor?' asked Mild. It was the first time Callie's mother had spoken.

'I was thinking the same thing.' Thern looked troubled.

'What's wrong?' Eve asked.

'The lakes of Trapor are in the heart of the Borderlands,' Callie explained. 'This is all forbidden territory for us – it's now the king's land where he and his army of rangers live.'

'Why would the unicorn go there?' asked Eve. She couldn't take her eyes off Ibid as he swished his tail lazily.

'The old stories say the unicorns roamed the Trapor Valley before the troubles,' said Thern.

'We want to help you, we really do,' said Oscar. 'What if Eve is the chosen one? What does the rest of the prophecy say?'

Thern recited:

'What you need runs down below:
Find the source to release the flow.
It takes one who is strong to tap into their power
And bring down the evil born of the tower.'

'I don't understand,' said Eve.

'Neither do we but if the first half of the prophecy can come true then the second half can too.' Thern looked at Eve. 'Will you help us?'

'Alright,' Eve decided. 'We're in. Let's head

33

to the lakes of Trapor. But first you have to get me out of this dress.'

Callie laughed. 'I love your bright dress! But yes, not very practical for a desert crossing. We will get you some of our handspun silks.'

Eve's face lit up at the idea of being dressed in the beautiful cloth. The girls fell into a conversation about dresses. Thern and Oscar exchanged a glance. *Girls!*

Eve and Oscar were soon dressed head to toe in the soft desert robes. They looked almost identical in the layers which would protect them from sunburn and windburn, and help them keep warm at night. The cloth was woven by Mild and was very soft.

After a hearty meal of root vegetables and rich spices which tasted delicious, Eve's tummy felt so full she was tempted to lie down and sleep.

Thern had other ideas. 'We must leave now, while the night protects us.'

Eve shook herself awake. It was going to be a long night.

**

It was an odd group that set out from Callie's community, leaving a small trail of footprints in the sand: Callie, Eve and Oscar, then Thern with Ibid close beside him. Callie travelled with her guardian animal, an elegant but wiry cheetah named Otto.

'I'm not sure which makes me more nervous,' Oscar whispered to Eve, 'heading into forbidden territory to find a unicorn and overthrow a king, or the fact that we are walking next to a wild panther and cheetah.'

Eve shot him a look. 'For once, I agree with you.'

They walked all night. Eve marvelled at Thern's ability to find his way using only the stars as their map. The endless rolling hills of sand looked the same to her. As dawn was breaking Thern allowed them to stop and get a few hours' sleep. Eve lay down and sank into an exhausted slumber.

It felt like only minutes had passed before Eve was startled awake by Ibid growling. The cat had slept beside her. She had felt strangely comforted.

'Crows!' Thern yelled as he shook Callie and Oscar awake. 'Stay hidden. I will lead them away.' He ran up the steep slope they had rested against. Ibid sprang after Thern but Thern ordered the panther to stay with Eve.

Callie leaped into action and threw her pale-coloured cloth over them all, including the cats. It acted as a cover and they blended into the sand.

'Lie low and keep still,' she ordered as she pulled the camouflage over their heads.

'What's going on?' asked Eve in a low voice.

'Crows are spies for the king,' explained Callie. 'If one of them sees us then rangers will be sure to follow.'

'Rangers?' asked Oscar.

'The rangers are the king's army. If they catch us they will make us slaves and turn us into rangers,' replied Callie, 'and we don't know of anyone who has ever escaped. Once a ranger they wipe your memory so that you forget your life, family and friends.'

'That sounds horrible,' whispered Eve.

Oscar and Eve lay still and waited. The only sound was the cats' rapid breathing. Eve listened anxiously but heard nothing until the muffled sound of horses' hooves galloping hard grew faint. Shouts rang out over the dunes but were soon replaced with silence.

Callie disappeared and returned a few minutes later looking upset.

'My father is gone,' Callie said quietly, her eyes filled with tears. 'The rangers have taken him.'

$\mathcal{E}$ ve put an arm around Callie and tried to reassure her friend.

'It will all be okay,' comforted Eve, although her words felt hollow.

'What do we do now?' asked Oscar.

'Go after them,' Callie wiped the tears from her face with a determined look. 'We can follow their tracks.'

It took the rest of the day to reach the

Borderlands. They passed a few people but they avoided eye contact and nobody spoke. 'Everyone suspects everyone else of being a spy for the king,' explained Callie.

Eve was amazed to see that each person travelled with an animal just as Callie did. Men and women walked alongside tigers, leopards, bears and even an elephant.

Finally they reached the wall which separated them from the Borderlands and the lakes of Trapor. Eve couldn't believe her eyes.

The wall was the size of a huge skyscraper stretching at least twenty storeys high. Its length spanned as far as Eve could see in either direction, a huge dark scar cutting across the land. Eve was reminded of the Great Wall of China, which she had learned about in geography.

'You're kidding!' Oscar objected. 'There's no way we can get over *that*.'

'We have to,' stated Callie firmly. 'We have to find my father. He is a proud man. I fear he might die before he bows to the evil king.'

'Well, we can't climb it,' Oscar said as he touched the smooth brick surface.

'There is no other way,' Callie replied stubbornly.

Oscar pulled out his Swiss Army knife. He stabbed the blade into the hard grout between the bricks in an effort to chip away at the barrier. The blade snapped. Not easily discouraged, Oscar tried to get a grip on the edge of the bricks and pull himself up. It was impossible to find a hold and he fell, landing on the sandy floor.

'Are you okay?' asked Eve.

Oscar nodded. 'It's hopeless.'

'Nobody has managed it yet and breakout groups of outliers have been trying for years.'

The trio sat glumly in the sand. Eve rubbed her palm and tried to think. Whenever she touched the mark on her hand it grew hot and a tingly feeling shot down her arm. Suddenly she had an idea.

'Callie!' exclaimed Eve. 'Tell me the next bit of the prophecy again.'

Callie spoke the lines:

'What you need runs down below:
Find the source to release the flow.'

'Water?' Oscar questioned.

'There is no more water,' Callie replied.

'Think back to the days when you had water here,' Oscar grew excited as he spoke. 'Was there a water channel or something like that? The wall could have been built on damp ground, you know, in a hurry. The brick could have eroded from the water before it all dried up completely.'

'It's worth a shot!' Callie's eyes lit up.

'Oscar,' exclaimed Eve, 'you're a genius.'

'You sound so surprised,' he teased Eve. 'I have my moments, even if I am a boy.'

Eve gave him a friendly punch on the arm.

'Follow me!' Callie began running. 'This way.'

The three friends, Otto and Ibid ran along the outskirts of the wall until they approached a dip in the land where Callie knew a creek had once flowed.

'Look for any weaknesses in the bricks!' cried Oscar as he ran his fingers along the rough wall, pushing at the bricks with all his might. The lower bricks were more vulnerable and the loose mortar crumbled. With a lot of effort one of the bricks loosened.

'I've got it!' Oscar shouted to the others. He began to furiously claw at the crumbling clay. The girls joined him and after a time

43

they had removed three bricks. A small gap was appearing but it was not yet large enough for a human or a panther to crawl through.

Otto let out a yowl and a hiss and butted his head against Callie's leg. He began to pace restlessly, his tail swinging fiercely this way and that.

'What is it, Otto?' Callie asked, turning to look at the sky. 'Crows!'

'Hurry!' Eve grabbed one of the loose bricks and used it to punch another one out.

'Nearly there,' muttered Oscar.

Callie threw her cloth over them all to hide their position while they continued to grapple with the hole. 'Quickly,' she hissed, 'they're getting closer.' She risked a peek out from under the cloth. She could see three crows circling nearby which meant the rangers were close.

Oscar worked furiously at the bricks and mortar until a large enough space had been created. He nodded to Eve. 'You try. Hurry!'

Eve lay down on her stomach and inched her body through the tiny space. It seemed too narrow for her shoulders but Oscar gave her a push and she just managed to pull herself out through to the other side.

'Come on!' Eve held out both hands and helped pull Callie through the tiny hole.

Next came the two large cats. Ibid was the largest but he managed to compress his body in such a nimble way that he made it through. He immediately joined Eve and stood next to her, panting heavily.

Finally it was Oscar's turn. They could hear the flap of the crows' wings. Oscar managed to pull his legs through and replace the cloth so the hole they had made was invisible to the naked eye. They were through.

'That was close,' panted Oscar as he picked himself up and gazed around.

'We're inside the wall,' whispered Callie. They all looked up and in the dimness they could see they were inside the hollow middle of the wall. A roughly paved road lit by burning lamps ran in each direction.

'Which way should we go?' Oscar asked Eve.

Eve closed her eyes and rubbed the mark on her hand. She felt a strong pull to her right and began walking. 'This way.'

It was creepy being inside the wall and Eve longed for the wide open space of the desert. It became harder to breathe the stale air and she felt as if the walls were closing in on them. It was with huge relief that she picked up on fresh air down a side tunnel which led out of the wall.

The contrast between the two sides of the wall could not be more marked. Here the vegetation was lush and tropical. Huge ferns shaded them like fans. Eve immediately realised she could hear the sound of birds chirping and insects humming. It was so different to the brooding silence of the desert.

'Try not to make a sound,' Callie said quietly as they began walking through the thick tropical undergrowth.

Otto and Ibid led the way through the jungle, making a rough path of trampled vegetation for the kids to follow. Ibid grew more and more distressed the further into the jungle they walked.

'Ibid is worried about my father,' Callie whispered. 'The connection between human and guardian animal is very strong.'

'Has it always been that way?' asked Eve.

'From what my father tells me it's how this world has always been. Having an animal guardian means protection for us. We were once able to move around safely. In return we helped the animals with the herbs we have grown for medicine, and by taking care of the land.'

'It's not like that in our world,' Eve said sadly. 'Many people treat animals badly.'

'Like the king,' agreed Callie. 'He wants it all for himself and doesn't care who gets hurt.'

They walked in silence for a little while.

'What's so special about these lakes, anyway?' asked Oscar.

'The story I have always been told is that it is a place of strong magic – unicorn magic. The king wants to take it for himself. He has the whole country and his ranger slaves but now he wants a unicorn.'

The thought of anyone harming a unicorn was very upsetting to Eve.

Then Otto and Ibid stopped. Otto let out a low snarl.

'What is it?' Callie asked as she stroked Otto's head. His tail swished angrily. Suddenly they heard the grunt of a ranger. 'Quick, hide!' Callie urged them.

They ducked down low among the ferns and watched.

'Thern!' gasped Oscar. Callie's face went deathly pale at the sight of her father. Ibid hissed and struck at the air with a clawed paw.

Thern was bound with rusty metal chains and flanked by rangers. The rangers looked frightening. They wore thick black armour and knee-high studded boots, and each of their faces was obscured by a black mesh shield.

'Shhh!' Callie held a finger to her lips. She indicated that they should follow the group.

Eve's fingers and toes tingled. Her palm grew hot and her face flushed. She looked around her. Through the ferns was a glittering pool of water and beside it stood a luminous figure. It was half-hidden by ferns but the glow of its coat was unmistakable. It radiated bright light.

'A unicorn,' breathed Eve. 'I have to warn it.'

She realised the others had gone after Thern. Eve felt torn but the pull towards the unicorn was too strong. She quickly threaded her way around the edges of the jungle until she was close to the unicorn.

'I mean you no harm,' called Eve in a low voice.

The unicorn shook its glorious mane and snorted. Tiny drops of glitter filled the air. Eve was close enough to feel the warmth of its breath on her skin. She held out the palm of her hand which clearly showed the unicorn mark.

'I think I brought you here,' Eve began. She hadn't known what to do but somehow she felt under a spell, as if she and the unicorn understood each other. 'We need to free the animals and the people and this land. We need your help. '

The unicorn stretched its neck towards Eve and lowered its head. Up close its horn gleamed. It was the whitest of whites. *Pure* was the word which sprang into Eve's head. This was a creature that couldn't harm anything or anyone.

The unicorn's soft lips nuzzled Eve's hand. 'You understand me, don't you?' she smiled.

A rustle in the bushes startled the creature. It threw its head back in alarm and whinnied.

'Quick!' cried Eve. 'Get away!'

The unicorn took off into the thick jungle and Eve turned around just as a pair of rough hands grabbed her. She gazed up into the dull, lifeless eyes of a ranger.

*E*ve was bound and led through the jungle to the base of a tower where, to her dismay, she saw that Callie and Oscar had also been caught. The kids were pushed through a narrow doorway and faced a steep staircase which led to the top of the tower. Eve strained against the ropes but it was no use. She was bound tightly.

At the top of the staircase they were

pushed inside a small cell. The ranger grunted as he slammed the metal door closed behind him.

There was silence as their eyes adjusted to the dark room.

'Hello children,' a croaky voice spoke from the dark corner of the cell.

'Father!' Callie cried. It was Thern, huddled in the corner.

'Are you hurt?' Callie asked.

'A sore head but nothing to worry about.' He gave his daughter a big bear hug.

'Ibid? Otto?' Thern asked.

'We think they got away,' said Oscar.

'I saw the unicorn,' said Eve.

'Did you speak with it?' Thern asked Eve urgently.

'I held out my hand and it understood me,' she replied simply. There was no other way to explain the amazing sensation of feeling so at one with a wild animal.

'You are our only hope.' Thern's eyes burned with intensity. 'Try to speak to it again.'

'Now?' Eve's face fell. 'But the unicorn could be anywhere … '

'Your power is strong. It will hear you.'

'I'm not sure I know how to.' Eve rubbed at her palm.

Callie took Eve's hand. 'Go back to the moment when you held your palm out to the unicorn,' she said gently.

'It snuffled me, and it tickled,' laughed Eve. She felt a warm glow at the memory. She looked down at her hand and her palm felt hot.

'Close your eyes and try to be in that moment,' said Callie.

Eve closed her eyes. She took a deep breath. In and out. The unicorn had smelled like a horse, but it was a pleasant smell. Its lips had been softer than she expected and the short bristles around its face had tickled her. In her mind's eye she was back there. She saw the trust in the unicorn's eyes, and she saw her palm begin to glow …

Eve's eyes shot open. 'The mark on my hand – it glowed when the unicorn touched me.' She looked down at her hand but it just looked like the imprint of the unicorn.

'That's something!' Thern encouraged her. 'Remember the final part of the prophecy:

It takes one who is strong to tap into their power
And bring down the evil born of the tower.'

'Come on Eve,' said Oscar. 'You can do this.'

Everyone was staring at her. Eve felt exhausted and scared. They had barely rested at all since arriving in this strange place and she hadn't eaten much. All of a sudden she felt faint. 'Leave me alone!' she cried, and sat by herself in the opposite corner of the dark cell. She leaned back against the wall and tears pricked at her eyes.

'It's alright Eve,' coaxed Oscar.

'I wish you had never made me go into the stupid attic,' Eve yelled at him.

'Nobody forced you to do anything,' Oscar snapped.

'I should have just played on my own,' continued Eve.

'Would have suited me fine!' snorted Oscar. 'Anyway, you're the *one* so you should be able to get us out of here.'

Eve shot Oscar an angry look. She glanced at Callie and Thern. They were still looking at her calmly and expectantly.

I'm not the chosen one – I'm just a girl, Eve thought. She felt completely overwhelmed. Her face grew hot and flushed. 'Oscar and

I did something we shouldn't have done and I picked up something I shouldn't have picked up, but I have no power. I'm plain old Eve McCarthy on holidays with my gran.'

Callie grabbed Eve's shoulders and held them firmly.

'It depends which eyes you are looking with.' Callie held Eve's gaze. 'To Ibid you are someone worthy of protecting. To me you are a stranger dressed like a princess with a mark which was foretold long before I was born. Can you try please? For us?'

Eve nodded and closed her eyes. She touched her palm and felt it grow hot. She saw the unicorn and the image was clear in her mind. All of a sudden another image flashed before her eyes. It was Mild leading a small group of desert nomads and their animals towards the wall. With a sick feeling Eve saw what was waiting for them.

It was the king and his enormous army of rangers!

Eve sucked in her breath at the image of Mild up against the army of evil.

'What is it?' asked Thern.

'We have to hurry,' Eve gasped. 'Mild is in danger.'

Thern's eyes widened in alarm.

Eve closed her eyes again and pictured the unicorn. 'We need your help.' She didn't say the words out loud. She thought them and that made them real. 'We need your help.' This time her lips moved as she spoke. 'We need your help.' Louder now.

Eve stood up, keeping her eyes closed and holding her palm out. 'We need your help,' she repeated, over and over again. Each time she said the words the palm of her hand glowed more brightly. She felt a warmth spread through her body and her hand grew hot.

'Eve … ' Oscar said uncertainly.

Eve's whole body was illuminated and a flash of brilliant light filled the room. Oscar ducked as Callie and Thern shielded their eyes.

When Eve opened her eyes the unicorn stood in front of her. With its head lowered and its trusting eyes upon her, it whinnied a welcome. Eve grabbed a fistful of mane and swung a leg over the unicorn's back.

She looked down at Oscar and Callie's astonished faces.

'Hurry,' she said reaching down to grab Callie's hand.

Thern, Callie and Oscar gripped each other tightly as they sat astride the unicorn's back.

'Hold on!' Eve called as a wind blew in the room. It swirled around them, sending objects flying through the air.

The ground shook as the unicorn reared up on its hind legs and whinnied. A flash of blinding light filled the cell and seemed to reach out to find all the corners of darkness within the kingdom. Eve could see it in her mind's eye. She could see the unicorn's magic at work.

Eve saw in one moment the entire history of a people and what had been taken from them. Then she saw Mild with Callie as a baby, with Otto guarding them. She saw the king arrive and take it all. She saw the land turn to desert, the wall being built. She saw a people defeated.

The next thing Eve saw was one man flanked by one hundred rangers.

'I've been expecting you,' he said.

Eve was looking at the king. She was no longer in the prison cell. The unicorn had brought them near the base of the wall, and they were standing between the king's army and Mild with her group of outliers. Thern and Callie ran to join Mild. Oscar stayed beside Eve and the unicorn.

'You walked right into my trap,' the king chuckled. 'You have brought me the unicorn.'

The unicorn reared up on his hind legs in protest. Eve clung on.

'Didn't you know?' Eve called from astride

the unicorn. 'There's a prophecy and you lose!'

The king sneered.

'Take them!' the king roared to his army of rangers. The rangers began to run towards them, their armour glinting in the sunlight. The air was filled with the sound of their heavy tread and grunting.

The nomads stood firm. Their group looked so small against the sea of rangers advancing.

'Now!' Eve channelled the power of the unicorn. She felt the magic pouring through her body. She was no longer just Eve McCarthy; she and the unicorn were one.

The leading group of rangers stopped. The unicorn magic had restored their memories, and they looked around in confusion. Suddenly they were men again and they had no idea where they were or what had happened.

The king looked furious. But half of his ranger army remained loyal and continued to charge towards them.

'What do we do?' Oscar cried.

'We have to believe,' said Eve.

A ranger ran up alongside the unicorn and knocked Eve to the ground. She lay winded as the ranger bore down on her. As she braced herself for the blow, a black blur flew through the air and knocked out the ranger.

'Ibid!' she cried. The panther looked at her and swished his tail playfully. She saw Otto and a host of other animals join in the fight. Animal guides who had lost their humans to the king's ranger spell came running from all directions, and it was they who broke the curse. Their magic was stronger than the king's and soon every ranger had regained his memory. The army was gone.

Eve drew in a deep breath. It was over. They had brought down an army and freed the land. They had won.

Everything the king and his rangers had built was no more. It wasn't destroyed, it wasn't rubble. It was just as if it had *never been.* In an instant the world of Panthor was restored. It was desert no more but was returned to the lush vegetation it had always been. It was filled again with animals and humans living together as one – guardians and protectors of each other.

***

The king stood between Ibid and Otto.

Thern spoke. 'You have not respected the laws of this country, the laws of nature, of living in harmony with the land with the native animals. Your penance will not be death or banishment. Instead you will live here among us. You will tend to the crops, you will plant vegetation. You will feed and nurture animals.'

'Like a slave!' spat the king. His words shot out of his mouth like venom.

'A slave to helping others,' Thern retorted. 'This is how we live. The only other alternative is to go with the unicorns but I'm not sure they will be as generous.'

The king looked up at the majestic being and shook his head. 'I will serve,' he said in a small voice. He seemed to shrink before their eyes.

'How can you trust him?' asked Oscar.

'Every living being in this world will be watching him,' Thern answered. 'I don't think he'll risk putting a foot wrong.'

Eve dismounted. She pressed her face against the unicorn's flank and breathed in its warm scent.

'Thank you.' She didn't say the words out loud. She didn't need to.

ve and Oscar spent time with Callie and her family in their treehouse village. The villagers built a treehouse for Oscar and Eve to say thank you. They were so excited to show them the special sites in Panthor. It was a beautiful place.

Eve spent as much time as possible with her unicorn. At first she was anxious to get home but soon she understood that although many days had passed here in Panthor, no time had passed in her home. Her parents would never know she had been away. It was a huge relief.

Eve and the unicorn had many adventures. They flew across the plains and swam in the lakes of Trapor. Eve met other unicorns who no longer stayed hidden in the fringes. They joined the world and learned to trust again.

Eve and Oscar met many of Panthor's people and their animals, and were welcomed wherever they went. However, the time came when the friends yearned for home.

Callie could tell. 'We know you only stay here because you are worried about us. It's okay. You need to go back to your own families.'

Eve hugged her friend. 'I'll miss you.'

Callie took Eve's hand and opened it. The

mark of the unicorn was still there. She traced it with her finger.

'I'll miss you too.' She nodded to Oscar. 'Look after her.'

Oscar rolled his eyes. 'If there's anyone who doesn't need looking after, it's Eve.'

'Ready?' Eve asked him.

Oscar nodded. 'Ready.'

The hardest part for Eve was saying goodbye to the unicorn, but she felt that he would always remain with her. She looked down at her hand and thought of home. Home with her parents, home with her gran. She grabbed Oscar's arm and closed her eyes.

***

The sick falling feeling didn't get any better on the return journey and Eve and Oscar landed on the floor of the attic with a loud thud.

'Ow!' exclaimed Oscar. This time the landing had hurt.

As he rubbed his leg he looked around. They were wearing their dress-up clothes, and the room was just as they had left it – except for one thing. The chest was closed and padlocked. It was as if their adventure had never happened.

'It did happen, didn't it?' Oscar asked Eve.

She held out her palm to him. The faint imprint of the unicorn remained on her palm.

'Your gran's going to kill us,' said Oscar.

'Tell me something I don't know,' muttered Eve.

They found Eve's gran sipping tea at the kitchen table. She looked as if she had only just woken up from her afternoon nap. Eve glanced at the calendar on the kitchen wall.

It seemed incredible but it was still turned to the date that they had gone into the attic.

Eve took a seat and Oscar followed her lead.

'Hello Eve,' said Gran. 'Oscar.'

Oscar stared down into his lap. 'Mrs Paterson,' he mumbled.

'Gran, I have a confession to make,' said Eve.

Her grandmother raised an eyebrow but said nothing. Eve had no choice but to continue.

'Oscar and I went up to the attic. I'm really sorry. I know it was wrong.' Eve looked down at the teapot, the tea-cosy – anywhere but her gran's eyes which she knew were boring a hole into her.

'Did you open it?' asked her gran, sitting up straight.

Eve nodded.

'Is it over?'

Eve nodded again.

Her gran sat back in her seat. 'That's powerful magic. You could have been hurt.'

Eve breathed a sigh of relief. Everything was going to be okay. Her gran understood.

She took another sip of her tea. 'That old wooden box is best kept away from children.'

'Old wooden box?' asked Oscar. 'Er ... you mean that metal chest with a padlock on it?'

Eve's gran shrugged. 'I don't know anything about that. I just wouldn't have wanted you near the Chinese wooden box, that's all.'

Eve locked eyes with Oscar.

'No way,' he mouthed back, shaking his head. Oscar had had enough adventures for the time being.

Eve winked at him. Oscar, she had decided, was okay.

For a boy.

Now available in the series

For more riddles and
adventures visit
www.keeperofthecrystals.com.au